BELIEVE

A Poetry Collection

Denise Alicea

"I have loved the stars too
fondly to be fearful of the night."
— Sarah Williams

CONTENTS

RISE

When the hurricane winds howl at your door,
Rise Up.

When the storm clouds gather and the rain pours,
Rise Up.

When the waves crash against the shore,
Rise Up.

When the darkness threatens to engulf you whole,
Rise Up.

When the cruel, cruel world takes its toll,
Rise Up.

For within you lies a strength that cannot be broken,
A courage that cannot be stolen or taken.

Stand tall and face the storm with all your might.
Know that you will emerge from the darkness into light.

For when the hurricane winds howl against your door,
You always have the power to rise once more.
Appreciation

Thank you for being who you are
Each and every day.
When I need a shoulder to cry on,
Someone to hear me,

You're always there.
You are an inspiration,
Someone to aspire to,
An admiration,
An angel.
Amidst the chaos and madness,
All the dark that this world holds,
Your presence and smile lights up every room.
You'll live forever in my mind and in my heart.
You will never be forgotten.

HELEN

With you, love had no expiration date.

A beautiful soul overflows,

kindness and generosity in endless measure.

Your memory will be embedded in my heart,

In every cavity of my chest.

I'll never forget what you made love sound like.

Oh Helen, I will never forget you.

FRIENDSHIP

Friendship is like a flower in full bloom.
It grows, yes, it grows.
It's beautiful, yet dangerous.
Nothing can stop or split this friendship.
It can withstand every disaster,
Every trial across space and time.

As we age,
It continues to blossom and grow.
As it grows, it becomes more beautiful
More beautiful than anything in its sight.
Its warmth, its protection, its love…

What a wonder, friendship.

THE TRODDEN PATH

Where angels walk, we follow.
Imagination fills our eyes.

Angels give us hope,
Bringing messages of peace and comfort,
Mending what was broken.
Angels dry the tears away.

The next time you feel alone,
Feel a touch on your shoulder,
The divine hand that soothes you.

It's the angels guiding you,
Through the dark and the light,
Their love and grace surround you,
No more need to fight.

Where angels walk, we follow,
Their wings a shelter from the storm,
Their voices a soothing balm,
When our hearts are broken, worn.

So let us walk with angels
On this journey called life.
Their presence a constant reminder:
We're never alone in our strife.

For where angels walk, we follow,
And in their footsteps, we can find
A path of love and compassion
That will guide us for all time.

BELIEVE IT

In the darkness, be a beacon,
A light shining bright.
When you think things are impossible,
Believe in all things kind.
When the seeds of hatred are sewn,
Plant seeds of hope.

Let your kindness and love show,
Help others learn to cope.
In the chaos, be a calming voice,
In the storm, be a shelter.

When the world is lacking choices,
Be an advocate for what is better.
In times of despair and strife,
Be a symbol of peace and goodness.

With every step you take,
Let empathy be your guide,
Let togetherness drive your mind.
In the darkness, be a beacon of light,
And let your actions shine.

WE CAN

When the world goes dark, shine a light.
When the winds of chaos come, stand your ground.
Let the hope be your beacon, your guide.
Don't let fear and doubt collide.

For in times of turmoil,
It's the strength of our resolve that keeps us.
When the tempests rage and the storms howl,
Stay firm and resolute.
Keep your courage, keep your smile.

Though the world may seem bleak and stark,
Shine your light bright, ignite a spark.
For in the darkness, there's always a glimmer,
And with your steadfastness, you'll help others to cope.

So, stand your ground when chaos reigns!
Let your light shine through the darkest of pains.

EMPOWERING ME

I walk with all the women of the ages,
Legendary Queens of times past.
Women who would not sit down,
Who would not fall victim,
Who would not give in,
Who would not waver.

I am a warrior in my own right,
With fire burning in my soul
I stand up for my beliefs.
My voice will not be silenced.
My spirit will not be tamed.

For I have a message to share,
A story that needs to be heard.
That story and I will not back down.
I will not be deterred.

My strength is not in muscles
Or the weapons that I wield,
But in the power of my words
And the passion that I feel.

I stand with all who came before
And all who will come next,
For we are the daughters of the earth.
Our voices matter.

Let the winds carry this message for me,
Across mountains and seas:
I will not be silenced.
I will be heard. I will be seen.

CREATION MYTH

We all come in different shades and colors,
Though we share the same Earth.

We may speak different languages,
But we share the same blue sky.

We come from different cultures,
But when we stand together,
We create an unbreakable bond,
Something strong and necessary.

In our unity lies our strength,
Our power to make a change,
To build a world that's just and fair,
Where everyone's voice is heard the same.

So let us come together, hand in hand.
Let us strive towards a brighter tomorrow.
For when we work together,
Moving towards a common goal,
We create a world without sorrow
A better world,
One for all of us together.

FURRY ANGELS

Furry angels, pure and bright,
Gentle creatures of the night.
Soft as feathers, warm as love,
Sent from heaven up above.

With eyes so big and hearts so kind,
Furry angels, they remind
Me of all that's good and true,
all the joy that life can bring too.

These furry angels, full of glee,
Bring comfort, peace, and grace
To those in need.
Their paws so gentle, their fur so fine,
Furry angels, so divine.

The beauty of the animal kind
And the love that we can find—
Let us cherish furry angels!
And all the joy they bring to our tables.
For they are truly heaven-sent,
Precious, a perfect augment.

LOVE FROM A DISTANCE

Until I see you again,
my heart will ache with pain.
The thought of you so far
brings tears to my eyes each day.

I long to hold you close,
to feel your warmth,
love you the most.
But for now, I must wait and yearn,
until the day when you return.

For now, I'll just hold onto memories
of laughter, joy, sweet melodies.
I'll cherish each moment we shared,
our love, our trust, always there.
And though the distance may be great,
our love will never dissipate.
For every beat of my heart does say,
I love you more with each passing day.

Until I see you again my love,
I'll send my thoughts through the skies above.
Hopefully they'll reach you, wherever you roam,
and guide you safely back to our home.

DREAMSCAPE

In the dream world, there's a place we go
Where the colors are bright and the rivers flow,
Where the sky is endless and the clouds are soft.
The wind whispers secrets, no matter how oft.
In this dream world, we can fly like birds
And speak with beasts, know every word.

We can walk on water and dance on air,
Travel to places as though we've always been there.
In our dream world, the impossible is true,
And the most wonderful sights are just within view.

We can meet the heroes of ancient tales
Or ride unicorns, with their rainbow trails.
In this dream world, there's magic all around.
Anything is possible, and nothing's bound.
It's a place we visit when we close our eyes.

Where we find new adventures beneath the skies.
So, let us journey to the dream world tonight
And explore its wonders in the soft moonlight.
In this realm of fantasy and play.
We can be anyone, go anywhere, each and every day.

TEAR DOWN THESE WALLS

Haven't we had enough of war?
We hurt ourselves and others,
Offer pain to all who cross us.

Haven't we had enough of tears?
Of shattered dreams for sisters and brothers
Fighting each other? Unable to see
That peace and love are all we need?

Let us lay down our weapons and our hate.
Let us embrace our common humanity,
With kindness and compassion serving as our fate.
Let us build a world of peace and unity.

For every life lost in the name of war
Is a precious gift that can never be restored.
Let us honor their memory and strive for
A future where each person knows they are adored.

Haven't we had enough of war?
Let us choose a different path, one where love is more.

TIME-JUMP

Flashbacks come unbidden, unannounced,
Memories from the past, once lost, now found.
They transport us to another time,
When life was different, when we were in our prime.

The sights and sounds come rushing back,
A flood of emotions we cannot stop.
The pain, the joy, the love, the fear,
All of them are returned and crystal clear.

We relive the moments, again and again,
As if we're really there, back in time.
The people we've known, the places we've been,
All of them appearing, as if in a dream.

Sometimes the flashbacks are happy and bright,
Filled with laughter, love, pure delight.
Other times, they're dark and full of sorrow,
Bringing back memories we'd rather not borrow.

But regardless of the type, they're each a part
Of who we are, where we came from, heart to heart.
They shape us, mold us, make us whole,
The past and present, our story told.

So let the flashbacks come, and let them go,
They are a part of us, a feature of the show.
Embrace them, learn from them, and let them pass,
They are the memories that make us last.

FINDING WHAT'S TRUE

Confusion, a state of mind
Where clarity is hard to find.
A tangle of thoughts, a web of doubt,
A state that leaves you wandering about.

A twisted maze with no end in sight.
Still, you try to navigate with all your might.
Yet every turn leads to a dead end,
Leaving you lost, no kindness, no friend.

You search for answers, but they elude,
And the questions continue to be renewed.
You try to grasp, but it slips away,
Leaving you helpless, day after day.

In this perplexity,
You long for something clearer,
A glimmer of light, a ray of hope,
To guide you through this slippery slope.

And then one day, it all makes sense,
A veil is lifted, you feel immense.
The confusion fades, and you can see,
The path ahead, clear as can be.

So, hold on, dear heart, and don't despair,
Confusion is just a fleeting affair.
And though it may seem like an endless night,
The dawn is just around the corner.

ABSENCE

In the silence of an empty room,
A sense of absence starts to loom,
A void echoes through the air
And leaves behind a deep despair.

The chair where once you used to sit
Now stands empty and alone.
The space you occupied before
Is now a vacuum, nothing more.

The memories of your presence
Now haunt this place, always so near.
Even now, your absence is so real,
A wound that time can never heal.

The sound of your voice is disappeared,
No laughter or jokes to fill what's cleared,
The emptiness that's left behind,
A weight upon my heart and mind.

And though you're gone, you're not away,
Cause I remember day by day.
Though your presence is not here,
Your essence lingers, oh so clear.

Yes, though you may be far away,
Your love remains, it's here to stay.

GRACE

Angels, ethereal beings of light,
Radiant guardians of the night,
Their wings spread wide, in flight they soar,
Watching over us forevermore.
With gentle grace, they guide our way
Whispering words, all they must say.

Their love and compassion, their divine embrace,
Helping us along at life's turbulent pace.
Angels, messengers of hope and peace,
A presence which brings a sense of release.

They lift us up when we're feeling low
And help our hearts to overflow.
In times of trouble, they lend a hand.
Their heavenly guidance helps us understand.

We are never truly alone,
For their love and protection is always shown.
Oh, Angels, you bless us from above
And fill our hearts with divine love.

PAST LIVES

In past lives lived, we were not who we are.
We wore different skins, we shone a different star.
Our stories, woven with love and strife.
From birth to death, a journey of life.

Some were kings and queens of old,
Their tales of power and glory foretold.
Others labored in fields and mines,
Their lives forgotten by the passing time.

We were warriors, poets, lovers too,
Sometimes villains, with hearts untrue.
Our past lives are a tapestry, rich and grand.
A legacy of the world, still at hand.

Though we can't remember all we've been,
Our souls carry the weight of our past sins.
Yet hope remains for the lives ahead,
For building anew with love instead.
In each life, we have the chance
To break the chains of past circumstance,
To shape our fate with every choice,
To live with purpose, to hear our own voice.
So let us honor the lives before
And learn from the wisdom they keep in store.
Then, we'll journey on, towards the light,
With hearts full of love and souls shining bright.

FAITH

Faith is the wings that help us fly,
The wind beneath our dreams to soar high,
A bridge that spans the gap of fear,
A refuge that shields us from life's tears.

It's a source of hope and healing,
A balm that soothes our troubled feelings,
A reminder that we're not alone,
And that we're loved beyond what may be shown.

Faith is a choice we make each day,
To walk in trust and not dismay,
To face each challenge with courage and grace,
To believe in the true miracles that come our way.

Hold on tight to this flame divine,
Let it light your path and shine.
For in faith, you'll find the strength to thrive
And the power to live a life that's truly alive.

SPIRITS

Spirits of the unseen world,
Mysterious and ethereal,
Whispering secrets, untold,
Invisible but ever real.

They dance among the shadows,
In the moon's pale, silvery light.
Their presence, though intangible,
Fills the air with magic and might.

Some are gentle, some are fierce,
Some are playful, some are wise.
All are bound by ancient laws.
All hold secrets in their eyes.

They whisper in the rustling leaves,
murmur in the evening breeze,
And though we cannot see them,
Their presence, one we can feel with ease.

They are the spirits of the land,
The sky, the sea, the fire,
And though they may be out of sight,
Their power lingers day and night.

When you hear the rustling leaves
Or feel the wind against your sleeve,
Remember that the spirits roam,
And you are never quite alone.

PUERTO RICO

Puerto Rico, my island home,
Where the sun shines bright and warm.
Beaches of sand and turquoise seas,
A paradise that fills my soul with peace.
The sounds of salsa and reggaeton
Echo through the streets all night long,
As people dance and sing with joy,
This vibrant culture that I so adore.

The mountains rise up to the sky,
A lush green landscape of pure delight,
With waterfalls and rivers,
Nature's beauty, a wonder to behold.
But the heart of Puerto Rico lies
In the spirit of its people, strong and wise,
A warmth and kindness that's hard to find,
A love for life that fills my heart and mind.

Puerto Rico, my island home,
Where my roots run deep and strong,
I am forever grateful to this place
And the memories it holds.

STAYING POWER

To remain in someone's heart,
A love that never truly departs,
A memory that lingers on,
Long after the moment itself is gone.

It's a feeling that's hard to describe,
But it's one that we all hope to imbibe.
To be cherished in another's soul
Is a love that makes us feel so whole.

For even when we're far apart,
Our love still beats within their heart.
A glowing flame that never dies,
Our love remains, despite goodbyes.

Let us cherish those we hold dear
And keep them close, always near.
For in their hearts, we will stay,
Even when we're far away.

RAGE

Rage, a fiery flame that burns,
A force that rages, a tempestuous din,
A storm that rages, a turbulent sea,
A hurricane that ravages, a fury free,

It rises up from deep within,
A primal force that knows no sin,
It boils and churns, it seethes and steams.
A tempest that builds, a rage extreme,

It's born from pain, from hurt and fear.
From loss and grief, from wounds severe,
It's fed by anger, by bitterness, hate.
A venom that poisons, a corrosive fate.

It lashes out, it strikes with force.
It rips and tears, it takes its course.
It burns and sears, it leaves a scar.
A mark that lasts, a raging star.

But rage can also be a force for good,
A passion that drives, a strength that should
Be channeled. Rage can be controlled.
A flame that warms, a heart that's bold.

Let it burn, let it rage and roar!
But use it wisely, let it not destroy.
For rage can be a power, a force divine.
A light that shines, a hope that's more than fine.

HOPE

Hope is a flame that flickers bright,
A ray of sun in darkest night,
A whispered promise in the ear,
That everything will be all right.

It's what keeps us moving forward still,
When life seems to be all uphill,
And though the road may wind and turn,
Hope helps us make the journey still.

With hope in heart, we dare to dream,
To reach for stars, to cross the stream,
To face the challenges ahead,
And rise above them like hot steam.

It's what makes life worth living for,
believing in something more.
To know that even in the dark,
Hope can light the way once more.
Hold on tight to hope, my friend,
And never let it come to end.

For with hope, we can overcome,
We can dream, we can transcend..

WALKING WITH A FRIEND

Walking with a person is a joy,
A simple pleasure, without any ploy.
The rhythm of our steps, in perfect tune,
Creates a sense of ease, soothing like the moon.
As we amble along, side by side,
Our conversation flows, a gentle tide.
Sharing stories, laughs, and tears,
We forget all our worries and let go of our fears.

The beauty of nature unfolds before our eyes,
As we stroll along, under the blue, blue skies.
The chirping of birds, the rustling of leaves,
Makes us feel alive.
As we walk, we observe and appreciate
The little things that we often underestimate.

The beauty of the flowers, the colors of the sky,
The warmth of the sun, the breeze passing by.
Walking with a person is more than just steps,
It's an experience.
It's a bond, that strengthens with every move,
A memory, that we'll cherish and keep.

Let's take a walk, you and I,
And let our worries pass us by.
Let's enjoy the moment and savor the pleasure
Of walking together,
A memory we'll treasure.

Latina Pride

With roots in the lands of the sun,
I proudly call myself Latina.
A mix of cultures, a fusion of colors,
My heritage, my identity, my persona.

From the Andes to the Caribbean Sea,
From the Amazon to the Mayan ruins,
My ancestors shaped this diverse land,
Their history engraved in my heart and hand.

I dance to the rhythm of salsa and merengue,
I savor the taste of tacos and empanadas,
I speak the language of Cervantes and Neruda,
I embody the spirit of Sor Juana and Frida.

I celebrate the fiestas of Dia de los Muertos,
I cherish the traditions of Semana Santa,
I honor the values of familia and comunidad,
I defend the rights of my gente and cultura.

In a world that often tries to divide,
I find strength in my Latinidad.
A bond that transcends borders and oceans,
A pride that shines like the sun in my soul.

So let me say it loud and clear:
Soy Latina, soy orgullosa.
I am Latina, I am proud.
I will always be.

LA ISLA BONITA

Puerto Rico, my beloved isle
Of sun and sea and verdant miles
Where mountains soar and rivers flow
And history's echoes softly glow.

Borinquen, land of Taino pride,
Where culture's blend will long preside,
A melting pot of Spanish flair
And African rhythms in the air.

San Juan's walls rise to the sky.
A fortress grand, a sight to spy,
El Morro stands with watchful eye.
O'er waves that crash and seagulls fly.

The coqui's call, a soothing sound
In rainforest's lush, emerald crown,
While salsa beats electrify
The night with energy and high

From Vieques' beaches to Culebra's isles
To El Yunque's trails and coffee piles,
Puerto Rico, my heart beguiled.
Beauty that cannot be defiled.

Honor this enchanted place,
And treasure all that makes it grace.
Puerto Rico, forever embraced,
your memory cannot be erased.

CATS

Cats, oh cats, so sleek and sly,
With eyes that gleam and fur that's nig,
They prowl and play, and oftentimes,
Their very presence feels quite divine.

They purr and rub and curl up tight,
On laps and beds, so warm and bright.
And though they're independent creatures,
Love fills our hearts when we see their features.

Their tails swish, their ears perk,
Their whiskers twitch, their claws definitely work.
Cats are a wonder, a joy to see,
Their grace and beauty, so wild and free.

From tabbies to Siamese,
All colors and patterns, big and small.
And though they may be fickle and proud,
Their company is something we cherish aloud.

Here's to cats, our faithful friends,
Whose presence in our lives never seems to end.
May they continue to grace us with their charm
And keep us cozy, safe from harm.

MOM

A mother's love is like no other,
A constant beacon, a guiding light.
Through thick and thin, she'll stand beside,
Her children's every triumph and strife.

She teaches us to walk and talk
And how to make our bed.
She shows us how to cook and bake
And tucks us in at night.

Her love is strong and ever true,
A bond that nothing can undo.
She cheers us on when we succeed
And wipes away our tears of grief.

She's always there to lend an ear
And offer sage advice,
She's our rock, our constant friend,
A guardian through all life's trials.

To moms, both far and near,
We honor and salute you,
For all the love you've given us
And the sacrifices too.

DREAMS

Dreams are like whispers in the night,
Softly spoken, often out of sight.
They come to us when we're at rest
And fill our minds with thoughts that crest.

They take us to another place,
A world of wonder, full of grace,
Where anything is possible
And magic is deeply probable.

In dreams, we can be who we want to be,
And do the things we thought we couldn't.
We soar up high and touch the stars,
And travel far, beyond all bars.

We meet the ones we miss so much
And feel their gentle loving touch.
We hear their voice, we see their face,
And if we're lucky, we feel their embrace.

Dreams can bring us joy and peace
And, sometimes, let our fears release.
They teach us things we need to know,
And help us grow and grow and grow.

So cherish your dreams each and every night.
Welcome them with open sight.
For they hold secrets, hidden schemes,
And take us to places beyond what they seem.

WEAR YOUR CROWN HIGH

With confidence and grace, I wear my crown high,
A symbol of my strength, a beacon to the sky.
It's not just a trinket, a mere accessory,
But a statement of my worth and my regency.

For I am a queen, the ruler of my life,
Of all the dreams and ambitions that will come.
And though there may be obstacles along the way,
I'll wear my crown high and seize the day.

Through trials and tribulations, I'll wear my crown high,
For my crown reminds me that I'm meant to fly.
I won't let doubt or fear hold me down,
For my crown is a symbol of my inevitable victory.

Let the world see me shine, let my light illuminate.
I'll wear my crown high, and I'll embrace my fate.
For I am powerful, and my destiny is mine.
With my crown held high, I'll continue to climb.

ENDLESS LOVE

In a realm where time has no domain,
Where passion's flame forever remains,
A tale unfolds of love's eternal reign,
A poem of never-ending refrain.

Across the cosmos, through celestial skies,
Two souls entwined, their spirits rise.
Through countless ages, their hearts align,
Held in a bond that knows no decline.

In the depths of darkness, they find the light,
A love that's fierce, yet still soft and bright,
Unyielding as the stars, open as the sky,
A symphony of love, sung all through any fights.

Through trials and storms, they hold on tight,
Their love a compass, guiding through the night.
Through battles fought and battles won,
Their love's foundation is solid as the sun.

They dance amidst the winds of change,
A dance that never knows estrange,
Their footsteps echo through eternity,
A testament to love's perpetuity.

Through whispered vows and tender kisses,
They etch their names on love's abysses.
Their souls entwined, forever they'll soar
In a timeless realm, each other they'll adore.

This tale of love unending
Inspires hearts, forever transcending.
For in this world of fleeting desires,
A love that lasts is what inspires.

ABOUT THE AUTHOR

 Born in Manhattan and raised in Connecticut, Denise Alicea started writing because drawing and painting simply weren't enough. A writer of poetry, romance, and children's books, Denise has won two awards for her short stories and received several finalist nominations. She loves technology, reading, and watching movies, and she spends much of her time managing her blog over at The Pen & Muse Book Reviews.

Website: http://denisealicea.com

Book Blog: http://thepenmuse.net

Join the newsletter:
https://www.subscribepage.com/z7p0o9

www.ingramcontent.com/pod-product-compliance
Lightning Source LLC
Chambersburg PA
CBHW070652130626
46555CB00006B/2830